A Note to Parents and Caregivers:

Read-it! Readers are for children who are just starting on the amazing road to reading. These beautiful books support both the acquisition of reading skills and the love of books.

The PURPLE LEVEL presents basic topics and objects using high frequency words and simple language patterns.

The RED LEVEL presents familiar topics using common words and repeating sentence patterns.

The BLUE LEVEL presents new ideas using a larger vocabulary and varied sentence structure.

The YELLOW LEVEL presents more challenging ideas, a broad vocabulary, and wide variety in sentence structure.

The GREEN LEVEL presents more complex ideas, an extended vocabulary range, and expanded language structures.

The ORANGE LEVEL presents a wide range of ideas and concepts using challenging vocabulary and complex language structures.

When sharing a book with your child, read in short stretches, pausing often to talk about the pictures. Have your child turn the pages and point to the pictures and familiar words. And be sure to reread favorite stories or parts of stories.

There is no right or wrong way to share books with children. Find time to read with your child, and pass on the legacy of literacy.

Adria F. Klein, Ph.D.
Professor Emeritus
California State University
San Bernardino, California

Editor: Jill Kalz
Page Production: Zachary Trover
Creative Director: Keith Griffin
Editorial Director: Carol Jones
Managing Editor: Catherine Neitge
The illustrations in this book were created digitally.

Picture Window Books
5115 Excelsior Boulevard
Suite 232
Minneapolis, MN 55416
877-845-8392
www.picturewindowbooks.com

Printed in the United States of America.

Library of Congress Cataloging-in-Publication Data
Jones, Christianne C.
The babysitter / by Christianne C. Jones ; illustrated by Zachary Trover.
p. cm. — (Read-it! readers)
Summary: Amy and Brad's parents go to the movies, leaving them with a babysitter who knows just what to do to make them happy.
ISBN 1-4048-1187-7 (hardcover)
[1. Babysitters—Fiction.] I. Trover, Zachary, ill. II. Title. III. Series.

PZ7.J6823Bab 2005
[E]—dc22 2005003901

Read-it! Readers
Purple Level

The Babysitter

by Christianne C. Jones
illustrated by Zachary Trover

Special thanks to our advisers for their expertise:

Adria F. Klein, Ph.D.
Professor Emeritus, California State University
San Bernardino, California

Susan Kesselring, M.A.
Literacy Educator
Rosemount–Apple Valley–Eagan (Minnesota) School District

PICTURE WINDOW BOOKS
Minneapolis, Minnesota

Mom and Dad are going to a movie tonight.

Amy and Brad have to stay home.

Amy and Brad feel sad.

They want to go to a movie, too.

Liz rings the doorbell.

Liz is the babysitter.

Liz wants to make Amy and Brad feel happy.

Liz has a great idea!

First, Liz makes popcorn.

Next, Liz pours lemonade.

Mil
Egg
Brea
ME

Then, Liz picks out a movie.

Finally, Liz dims the lights.

Amy and Brad enjoy their own movie theater.

Amy and Brad feel happy again.

Liz feels happy, too.

More *Read-it!* Readers

Bright pictures and fun stories help you practice your reading skills. Look for more books at your level.

Ann Plants a Garden by Susan Blackaby
Bess and Tess by Susan Blackaby
The Best Soccer Player by Susan Blackaby
Dan Gets Set by Susan Blackaby
Fishing Trip by Susan Blackaby
Jen Plays by Susan Blackaby
Mary's Art by Susan Blackaby
Moving Day by Susan Blackaby
Pat Picks Up by Susan Blackaby
A Place for Mike by Susan Blackaby
Room to Share by Christianne C. Jones
Wes Gets a Pet by Susan Blackaby
Winter Fun for Kat by Susan Blackaby
A Year of Fun by Susan Blackaby

Looking for a specific title or level? A complete list of *Read-it!* Readers is available on our Web site:
www.picturewindowbooks.com